'21

TO: EMMA

LOVE,
UNCLE JIM

Queen of the Kisses Meets Sam Under A Soup Pot

Love and Kisses to my children, Elanit and Aviva Kayne and my parents, Nat and Ruth Wolff—SWK

Special thanks to my family, friends and especially Grandma Brown-Dickson for her endless laughter and love—MB

Library of Congress Catalog#: 95-78160
Library of Congress Cataloging in Publication Data
Kayne, Sheryl W. Queen of the Kisses meets Sam under a Soup Pot
Summary: Sam, doesn't want her Grandma to leave after a family visit,
so she hides knowing her Grandma will not leave until she kisses
Sam goodbye. It takes the special magic and kisses of Queen Theresa to
find Sam and convince her that love and kisses are long lasting.
1. Children's Stories, American. [1. Kisses-Fiction]
1. Blonski, Maribeth, ill. 11. Title
ISBN# 1-880851-18-0

Queen of the Kisses
Meets Sam Under A Soup Pot

written by Sheryl Wolff Kayne • illustrated by Maribeth Blonski

Queen Theresa adds a teaspoon of
pucker powder to sweeten her morning tea
as she watches the rising sun kiss the Land
of the Kisses awake.

Suddenly the Emergency Kissing Siren
begins to howl: "Help Kiss! Help Kiss!"

Queen of the Kisses blows three kisses into
the air to activate Kissaroo, the kissing problem
detector.

"Kissa, kissa, mmwah, mmwah," Kissaroo warms up. "My my, Queenie, it's early in the day, kissa, mmwah. Kissaroo on line and ready."

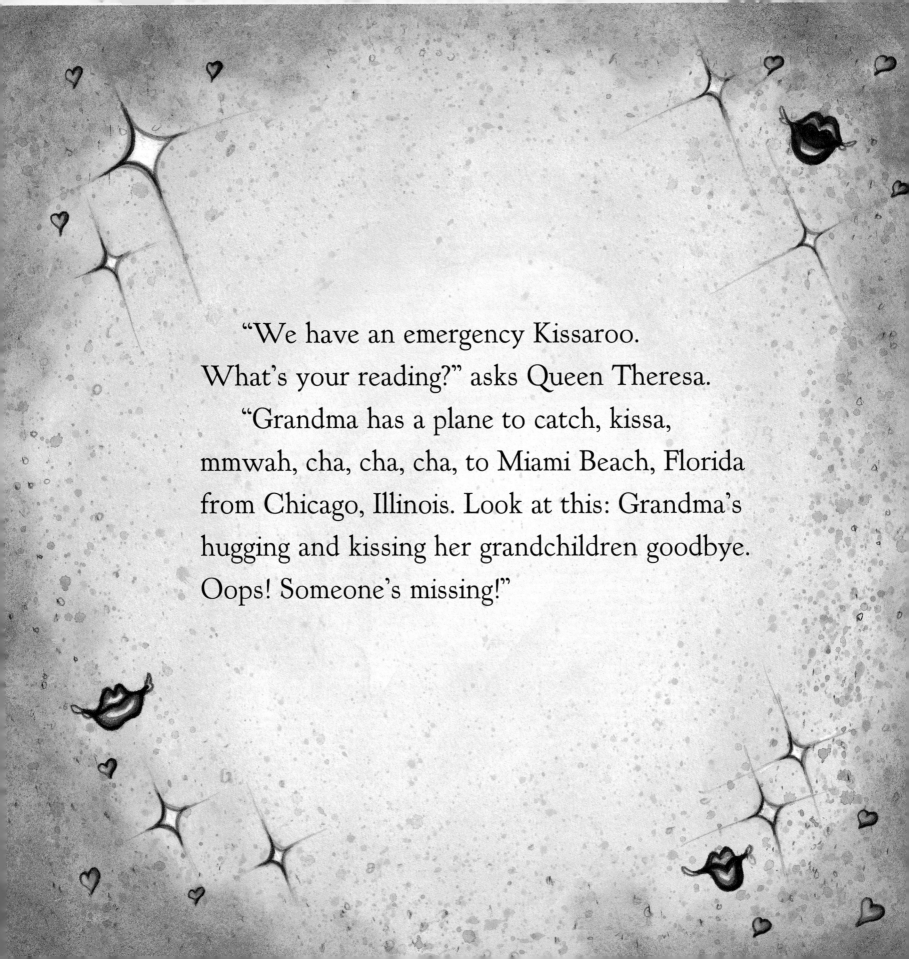

"We have an emergency Kissaroo.
What's your reading?" asks Queen Theresa.
"Grandma has a plane to catch, kissa,
mmwah, cha, cha, cha, to Miami Beach, Florida
from Chicago, Illinois. Look at this: Grandma's
hugging and kissing her grandchildren goodbye.
Oops! Someone's missing!"

"Check your backup screen, Kissaroo.
What's the problem?"

"Sorry, ma'am, no can find Sam," smacks
Kissaroo. "Grandma must deliver kiss, quickaroo.
No can do."

"Grandma's got a plane to catch," Queen Theresa mumbles to herself. She turns the Kissaroo control panels to check Sammy's room, the backyard, the kitchen. No Sammy.

Sammy's right shoe is next to her left shoe on the shoe shelf. Sammy's jacket is on the right hook in the coat closet. Sammy's blue cap is on the left hook. Where could Sammy be?

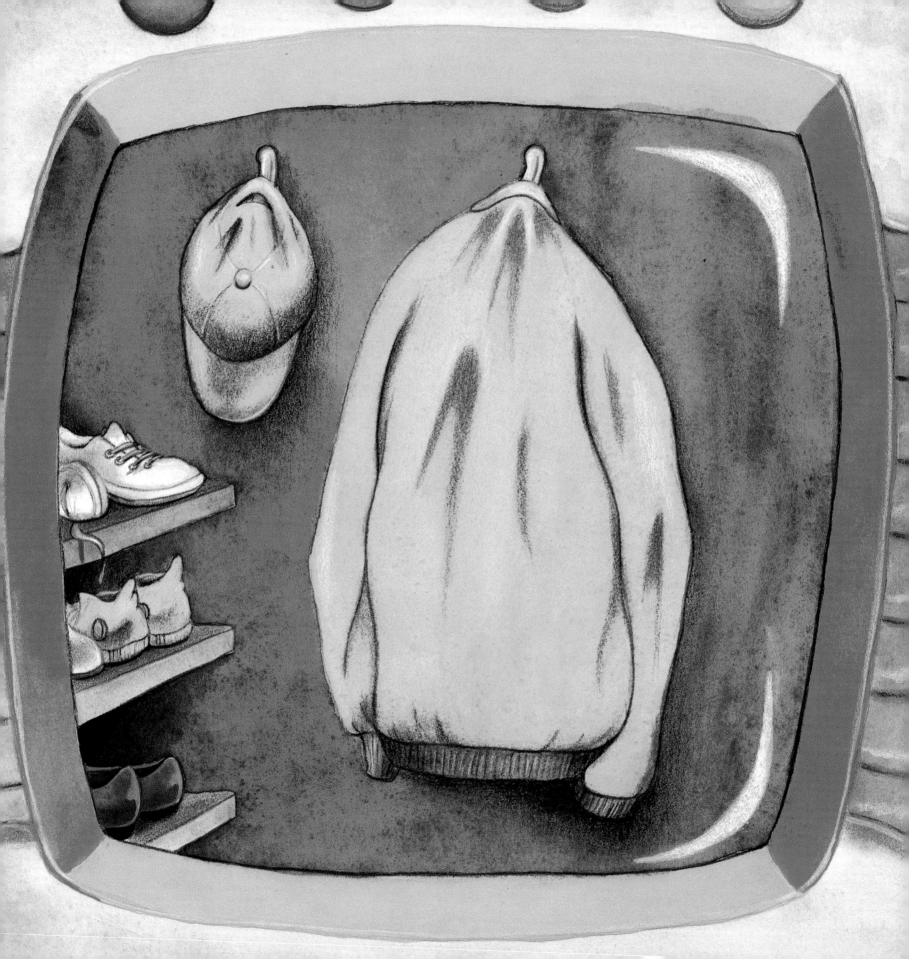

"This here's one humongo problemo," Kissaroo hums kissingly. "Granny can't shuffle off to Florida without kissing all of her grand-children goodbye. No kiss, no go, Granny-o."

"Kissaroo," wonders Queen Theresa, "how will I find Sam?"

"You won't if Sammy has anything to do with it," whistles Kissaroo. "Granny can't find her and she's going nuts!"

"So am I! Try harder Kissaroo, Grandma's got a plane to catch!"

"Mmwah, mmwah, smack, smooch, bee-bah-bop-a-boop. You won't believe this one, Queenie. Sam is out of sight! Whoa, she's hiding in a metal jacket."

"Kissaroo, there's no such thing as a metal jacket!" says Queen Theresa.

"Maybe it's aluminum," whirs Kissaroo. "Hey, hey, hey, presto chango. Sammy's hidden but good in a tunnel, or a cave, in the kitchen!"

"Sammy's getting real comfy there in that, uh, stainless steel soup pot! Sammy's hiding under a soup pot! Wow, am I good or what?"

"You're the best in the business, Kissaroo. Please program the microscopic telescopic transferential transportation transporter for Sammy's, 147 Hillside Avenue, Chicago. I'm on my way!"

"Oh, my goodness, it's crowded in here. I've never been under a soup pot before."

"Who are you?"

"I'm Queen of the Kisses. Sounds like you need some help."

"I don't need kissing help, if that's what you mean. I know how to kiss, see?" Sammy puckers up.

"Nice pucker. Sam, everyone is looking for you."

"I know," says Sam. "Grandma has a plane to catch. She wants to kiss me goodbye and leave. I just can't kiss my Grandma goodbye, so don't ask me."

"Sammy, kisses are to share, to give away. They are not for keeps. If you try to keep a kiss, it might be a pucker, or maybe even a kissy sound," Queen Theresa squeaks out a mmwah, "but until you give a kiss to someone you care about, it's not a kiss."

"If I give Grandma the goodbye kiss she wants, she'll go away." Sammy pulls the pot down further around her shoulders, making Queen Theresa shrink into a very teeny, tiny queenie.

Queen Theresa perches onto Sam's shoulder to whisper in her ear, "Sam, this is the magic of love and kisses. Grandma will leave you her kisses and she'll take yours with her."

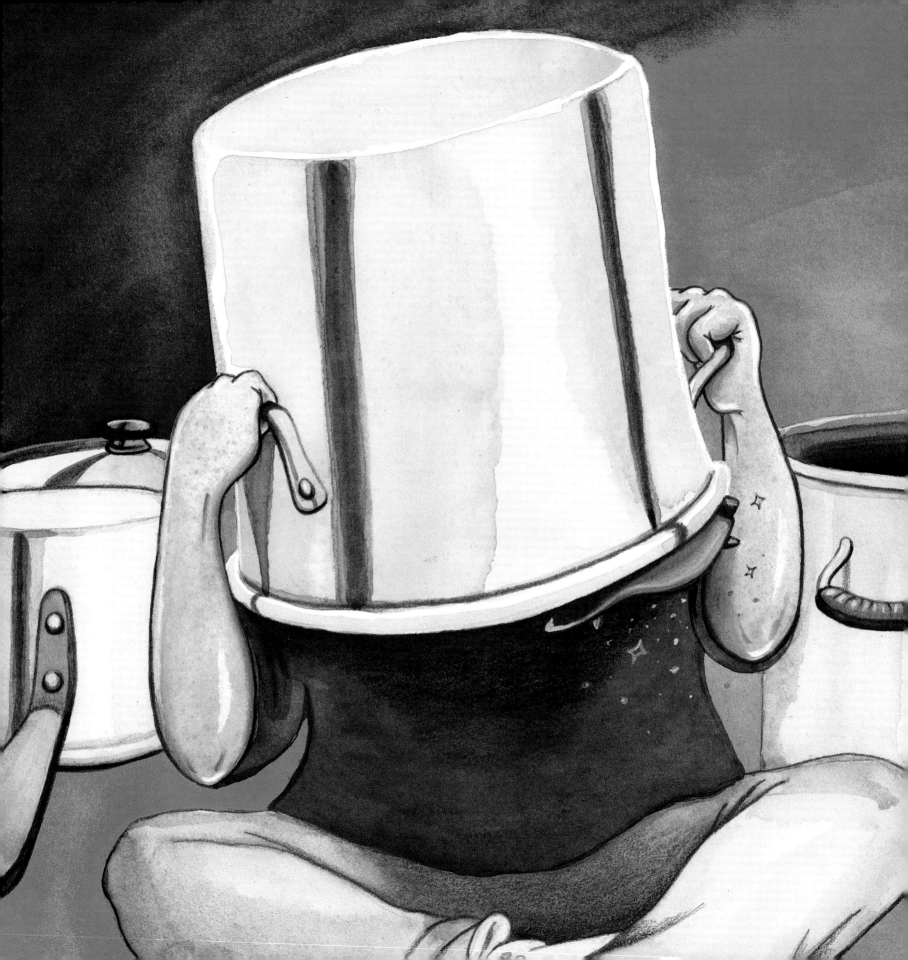

Queen Theresa puckers up while she
moves around the inside of the pot to gently
kiss Sam on the right cheek, then on the left.
Sammy pats her cheeks. "Your kisses feel
almost like Grandma's good morning kisses."

"Those kisses won't go away. They'll always be yours," Queen Theresa sprinkles Sam with an extra pinch of never-forget-the-one-you've-kissed kissy dust. "Soon you'll be seeing Grandma again and she'll fill up your supply over and over with even more hello kisses, I love you kisses, and you're the greatest kisses."

"Grandma's got a plane to catch!"
yells Sammy. She throws off the stainless steel
soup pot and tosses Queen Theresa a goodbye
kiss. Queen Theresa catches it with her lips.

Another job well done. Queen Theresa releases her flying kisses and see you later dust. The microscopic telescopic transferential transportation transporter sends her right back to the Land of the Kisses.

Queen of the Kisses sips her morning tea. It's kissingly just right.